This book belongs to:

....

....

Designer: Victoria Kimonidou
Editor: Matthew Morgan

© 2017 Quarto Publishing plc
The Old Brewery, 6 Blundell Street,
London N7 9BH, United Kingdom.
T (0)20 7700 6700 F (0)20 7700 8066
www.QuartoKnows.com

A catalogue record for this book is available from
the British Library.

ISBN 978 0 71124 108 4

Manufactured in Shenzhen, China HH112018

9 8 7 6 5 4 3 2 1

There's No Place Like Home

Dubravka Kolanovic

NEW BURLINGTON

William loved taking long walks

with his Mum and Dad.

And every evening, when the stars
appeared in the sky, his Mum and Dad
took it in turns to read him

a bedtime story.

One day, Mum and Dad shared some happy news with William.

Before long, a baby brother arrived. William was **very excited.**

But now Mum and Dad were busy all the time.

And when they forgot his bedtime stories, William was sad, as he thought his parents didn't love him anymore.

William wanted to find a new home.
So he picked up his book and left.

William found his friends, the ducklings, waddling through the forest. "What's wrong?" they asked.

"I'm looking for a new home," he said.

"Come with us to our lake," the ducklings said. "It's very pretty."

The lake was pretty, but William was worried about his book getting wet.

Next William met his
friend Little Mouse.

"Come with me to my
mouse hole," Little
Mouse suggested.
"It's very cosy."

Little Mouse's mouse hole was cosy, but it was far too small for William and his book to fit inside!

William then met his friend, Little Wolf.

"Come with me to my cave,"
Little Wolf said. "It's **big**
enough for both of us."

Little Wolf's cave was very roomy,
but it was too dark for William to read.

The sun was setting, and William
was still looking for a home.

He felt a friendly wing on his shoulder.

It was Owl! "Come to
my nest," Owl said.
"I LOVE reading!"

William followed
Owl, but when he
arrived at Owl's nest,
it was too high.

William felt lonely. It was dark, and he was scared. The stars appeared in the night sky.

He missed his home and family.
But just then, he heard some familiar voices.

It was Mum, Dad and his little brother!

"William, thank goodness you're safe!"

said Mum and Dad.

"Sorry for leaving," said William.

"Now I know there is no place like home, because home is where my family is!"

Even though it was
late when they got home,
William and his family did
not go to asleep right away.

After all, Mum and Dad
had to catch up on all the
bedtime stories he had missed.

Next Steps

Show the children the cover again. Could they have guessed what the story was about from looking at the cover? Read the title. Does the title give them a clue?

William loves going on long walks with his Mum and Dad, and having a bedtime story. Ask the children what they like doing with their family. What's their favourite bedtime story?

William's Mum and Dad are having a baby. Ask the children if they have any brothers or sisters. What do they think are the good things about having siblings?

William is sad when he thinks his parents don't love him any more. Do the children think leaving home was the right thing to do?

Little Mouse has a cosy mouse hole, but it's not right for William. What's wrong with it? Discuss what's wrong with the other animal homes William visits.

William ends up all alone in the dark, feeling scared and lonely. Have the children ever been away from home and missed their family?

William's Mum and Dad are pleased to find him. How do the children think William felt when he saw them again? What did his parents learn?

At the end of the book, William's Mum and Dad read him a bedtime story, even though it's late. Can the children remember any special times they have stayed up later than their normal bedtime?